Also by Ann Cameron

The Secret Life of Amanda K. Woods
More Stories Huey Tells
The Stories Huey Tells
More Stories Julian Tells
The Stories Julian Tells
Julian's Glorious Summer
Julian, Dream Doctor
Julian, Secret Agent
The Most Beautiful Place in the World

Gloria's Way

Gloria's Way

Ann Cameron
Pictures by Lis Toft

Frances Foster Books

Farrar, Straus and Giroux • New York

1 3 5 7 9 10 8 6 4 2

Library of Congress Cataloging-in-Publication Data
Cameron, Ann, 1943–
    Gloria's way / Ann Cameron ; pictures by Lis Toft. — 1st ed.
        p. cm.
    "Frances Foster books."
    Summary: Gloria shares special times with her mother and father
and with her friends Julian, Huey, and Latisha.
    ISBN 0-374-32670-3
    [1. Friendship—Fiction.   2. Parent and child—Fiction.   3. Afro-
Americans—Fiction.]   I. Toft, Lis, ill.   II. Title.
PZ7.C1427G1   2000
[Fic]—dc21   99-12104

To Lucette and Pierre Stitelmann,
dear friends and great adventurers

Contents

Gloria's Way

A Valentine for My Mother

I love my mom very much. If I could, I would give her everything beautiful. Gold and silver, diamonds and mountains. Palaces with towers, and every tower with a flag, and every flag embroidered with her name.

Lucy. I think it is the prettiest name in the world.

But I don't have gold or silver, or diamonds or mountains, or palaces with towers, or flags with her name to raise high in the air.

So I made her a valentine.

I went to the closet and found red, shiny wrapping paper. I got scissors and white paper and glue and markers from my mom's desk.

With the red paper I made a big heart. I cut holes in it to make five double doors. I glued a bigger white heart behind it. I cut the outside edge of the white paper into scallops with tiny holes in them, like lace.

Inside the first double doors of my valentine, I drew a picture of my mom and her smile. In the other double doors, I wrote a message.

> *I love you*
> *like the sky*
> *but*
> *MORE.*

The red paper doors closed over the message. You had to notice the red paper was cut to open it and see the words.

My mom would notice. She would open the doors carefully and read the words one by one.

I found a needle in her sewing box. I threaded it with red thread and pushed it through the top of the valentine. I made a strong loop. Then I took the valentine outside and tied it to the brass knocker on our front door.

My mom wouldn't be home for a long time yet. I did my homework. Then I read a book.

It was a windy afternoon. Bushes outside swayed and rubbed against the window. I wondered if my valentine was safe. I went to the door and opened it.

My valentine was in trouble! It was pulling on its thread, spinning like a top. I started to take it down and it made a ripping sound. It tore loose from the door. It flew.

"Oh no!" I shouted. I grabbed for it.

My valentine climbed the air like a shiny red

kite. It took huge steps into the sky. A long way off, it came down in the street, and then it rolled.

I ran after it as fast as I could.

"Stop! Stop!" I yelled.

It skimmed the street, sailing and sliding. It blew under a fence. It rolled into a yard.

In the middle of that yard there was a big cage. My valentine rolled into it.

The cage went from the ground to higher than my head. When I got to it, my valentine, all perfect except for its white edges, was lying right in front of me.

Above it, swinging on a metal ring, was a great big green-and-blue parrot.

"Hello," I said.

"Hiyeeeee!" screamed the parrot, loud, like a person in pain. Then it swung upside down on its ring, perfectly calm, like a circus performer.

It jumped to a horizontal bar right next to my head, so close I could see its ivory beak and the gleam in its yellow eye, the muscles in its scaly legs and all its claws like long, gray fingers.

"Blue and green feathers are very pretty together, I think," I told the parrot.

"No!" said the parrot, in a strange hoarse voice.

"Well," I said, "if *that's* the way you're going to be . . ."

I knelt by the side of its cage. I slipped my hand between the bars.

Curling and uncurling its gray claws, the parrot swung down the side of the cage.

I pulled my hand out of the cage.

"All right," I said. "Let's just talk."

But I didn't know what to say to a parrot. Tell the truth, I decided.

"I can never move as fast as you can," I admitted.

The parrot didn't answer. It opened its beak and then snapped it shut. Its beak was thick and strong and curved like a sword.

"Do you bite?" I asked.

"Don't bite!" the parrot said, in a woman's voice. "Don't bite. It's not nice!"

Somebody had tried to teach the parrot something. But maybe it had only learned the words, not the meaning.

I looked at the house set way back in the yard. Maybe someone was home.

I walked to the door and knocked. If somebody came, I would say, "Excuse me, but your parrot has my valentine."

Nobody came.

I went back to the cage. I had to stick my hand in fast and get my valentine. If I dared.

The parrot was on its ring again, swinging and fluffing its shining green-and-blue feathers.

"I want my valentine, that's all," I said.

"Guess again," the parrot said. Its throat puffed out and got big as a person's when it talked.

"What's your name, sweetie?" it asked.

"Gloria," I answered. "Gloria Jones."

It didn't say anything then. It just gripped the side of the cage and stared at me from the tiny black pupils of its yellow eyes.

"I'm Gloria Jones," I repeated, "and, like I said, all I want is my valentine."

The parrot looked puzzled and almost kind.

"Tomato? Tomato?" it said.

Up by its metal ring, it had a food tray that hung down from the ceiling on a pole. On the tray were two pieces of lettuce and a tomato.

"Big bird!" the parrot said proudly. It sounded just like a man. It jabbed its fierce beak deep into the tomato.

"Don't spill!" I told it.

Red juice spurted out. The parrot rolled its

head so far its eyes were on the bottom and its beak was on the top. It stretched its claws and straightened its head and looked for something more to bite. In words it didn't say anything, but with its eyes it did.

Maybe it meant, "Don't come into *my* yard and tell me what to do!" Or maybe it meant, "What I just did to the tomato, I can do to you!"

"I don't want your tomato," I said. "I just want my valentine."

I could tell that it didn't believe me.

It ruffled its feathers. They were shining, like velvet. Under its tail, some of them were red and soft blue.

"I am a friend," I said.

"Friend, friend, friend," said the parrot in a bored voice. It jabbed another hole in the tomato.

"Are you going to let me take my valentine?"

"Cleopatra! Cleopatra! No! No! No!" said the parrot, in its woman's voice.

"This valentine is not yours!" I said.

"Cleopatra! Cleopatra! I am Cleopatra," the parrot said, in its man's voice. It jabbed three more holes in its tomato. Big wet holes.

"I am not afraid of a bird," I said.

I stooped close to my valentine.

The parrot watched me with angry eyes.

"This valentine is for my mother!" I said.

I slipped my hand between the bars.

The parrot dove to the bottom of the cage.

I jerked my hand out.

The parrot flew up to its metal ring. It reached its left leg up and covered its eye with its foot. I could tell it was thinking, but I didn't know what.

It put its foot down on its tray.

"Tomatoes. Cleo likes tomatoes," it said.

"Sometimes," it added. And then it hit the tomato hard with its beak.

The tomato rolled to the edge of the tray.

It fell on my valentine like a bomb.

Tomato seeds were all over my valentine. Juice ran in all the little doors where the words were.

There was no use trying to rescue it. My valentine was ruined.

"Cleo is a good girl," said the parrot.

"I hate you!" I said.

I don't know what the parrot looked like then, because I couldn't see it, and I didn't care anyway.

I ran, and I just kept running. I didn't even know where, I was just running and crying and crying and running, and wiping my eyes with my hands.

I ran a long way. When I got out of breath, I was passing by Mr. Ralph Bates's car-repair place.

I know Mr. Bates. I have two friends, Julian and Huey, and Mr. Bates is their dad.

I didn't want Mr. Bates to see me crying. I walked fast to get by his place, but he saw me anyway.

"Hi, Gloria," he said.

I didn't say anything, because I couldn't.

"Gloria, honey, come here, what's the matter?" he said.

So I told him I had a valentine for my mom but I didn't have it anymore because of a parrot that had wrecked it, and it was the very best valentine I ever made.

Then I cried, and he hugged me and lent me his handkerchief.

I sat on the old couch in his office.

"Parrots have strange, interesting minds," he said. "But, Gloria, I hate to see your mind get messed up by somebody else's mind. Especially a parrot's."

"I hate that parrot!" I said.

"You had such a nice plan, Gloria," Mr. Bates said. "Are you going to just give it up?"

"I can't make another valentine," I said. "I don't have any more paper."

"I do," Mr. Bates said. "I have lots of paper."

He opened a drawer in his desk, and there it was, all nice and white.

"I have tape, too, and scissors. And a red pen," he said. "And I have a whole lot of old newspapers." He pointed to them, back in a corner.

"I don't know," I said.

"What don't you know?"

"If I make a valentine, I want it to be like the last one," I said, "and I don't have any red paper."

Mr. Bates looked thoughtful.

"I believe you could make a new valentine as good as the last one," he said. "Or better. Even without red paper. Of course, you'd have to forget about the parrot and all that. You'd have to get back to thinking about your mom."

I thought of my mom. I realized a strange thing. Everything that had happened was because I wanted to make her happy, but I was so mad I had forgotten about her!

"Instead of giving her red paper, you could give her special words," Mr. Bates said. "You could find words you like in the newspaper and cut them out, and mix them until they make a special message."

I looked at the newspapers in the corner. The first words I saw wouldn't make a good valentine. They were "war," "guns," and "death."

Mr. Bates was watching my eyes.

"You'd need to look in the back pages for the nice words. You could sit right here at my desk and look for them."

"Okay," I said.

We got a lot of newspapers. I sat down at Mr. Bates's beat-up old desk. He set the newspapers on top of it and reached into his desk drawer for a pair of scissors.

"Call me if you need me," he said. "You know where the raisins are."

In one corner of his office Mr. Bates has a rubber tree plant that grows so slowly it will be a thousand years before it grows an inch. That plant makes me feel calm.

On top of the filing cabinet is where Mr. Bates keeps the raisins. I took some, and I felt better.

Mr. Bates's office is a good place. It is a place where you can just be how you are, and even if you feel bad, that is okay, too.

There are good words in the newspaper if you look inside. On the "Society" page I found

"dancing." On the "Home" page I found "garden" and "raindrops." On the "Recipes for Today" page I found "honey." On the "Features" page, I found "bells." On the "Weather" page I found "clouds." And there were more good words. Even "mom."

I took Mr. Bates's scissors and cut the words out. I arranged them all different ways. I looked for the way that sounded the best. Then I made a big heart out of white paper and taped the words on it. I made drawings of red flowers all around the edge.

"Mr. Bates," I called. "I finished it!"

He came to look at my new valentine.

"It turned out nice!" he said.

He found a big envelope for me to carry it in, so the wind wouldn't tear it. I took a shortcut home, so I didn't have to go by the parrot. Maybe someday, when I didn't have a valentine, I would talk to it again.

When I got to our house, I didn't tie the valentine to our door knocker. I took it inside.

My mom would be home any minute.

I took my valentine out of the envelope and read it one more time.

The Promise

Latisha is my new friend. One day she asked me to play house.

"I don't want to," I said.

"Why?" Latisha asked.

"Because I never did," I said.

"Why?"

"Because Julian is my best friend, and he doesn't play house, so I don't."

"I'll ask Huey," Latisha said.

She went to find Huey, Julian's little brother. I went along.

"Huey, would you play house?" Latisha asked.

"I couldn't do that," Huey said.

"Why not?" Latisha asked.

"Because of my brother," Huey said. "If I played house, my brother would laugh at me."

"But maybe he would play house if I asked him," Latisha said.

"Don't even try," Huey said.

Latisha got angry. "I always play what you all want to play, but nobody will play what I want!" she said.

She went home.

We didn't even see her for three days.

Then she came over to my house. Julian and Huey were already there.

"Where have you been?" Julian said.

"Busy," Latisha said. "My dad got me a new playhouse."

"He did!" Julian said. "Can we see it?"

"Maybe," Latisha said.

"What do you mean, maybe?" Julian said. "We're your friends."

Latisha looked at us, thinking. "If you promise to eat apple pie when you come, you can play in it."

"All right!" we said.

"Do you promise?" Latisha said.

"Of course," we said. "We promise."

"Come at two," Latisha said.

We took Huey's dog, Spunky, with us to Latisha's house. Her new playhouse was in the back yard. It was white, with a high peaked red roof with little windows in it, and two more windows in the main room, and another room with a flat roof that would be good for jumping off.

The door had a fancy shiny gold key sticking in the lock.

We knocked.

Latisha opened the door.

"Come on in," she said. "Your pie is ready."

We went in. The first room had a table and chairs, just the right size for us, and a doll bed with a doll in it. Spunky sniffed into all the corners and wagged his tail.

"This is neat!" Julian said.

"Come on into the kitchen," Latisha said.

We went into the little room with the flat roof. It had a pretend stove and a pretend sink. Our pie was sitting on a low shelf under the window.

It didn't look like any apple pie I'd ever seen.

"Why do the apples look raw?" I asked.

"I baked the pie with sugar sprinkled on top, in my pretend oven," Latisha said. "My pretend oven only has pretend heat."

"Why is the pie so white?" Huey asked.

"I couldn't make a pie crust," Latisha said. "My mom won't let me keep butter here. She

says it will attract bugs. The crust part is just flour and water mixed."

"Flour and water mixed! That's paste!" I said.

"Paste can taste good. I tasted some at school once," Latisha said.

"Latisha, I don't want pie," Julian said. "I'm not feeling good."

"Me either," Huey said.

"I ate a very big lunch," I said. "I don't want any either."

"You all promised you would eat it!" Latisha said. "And it's good!"

"Maybe Spunky would like it," Julian said.

"Spunky, come! Smell this pie!" Huey said.

Spunky walked up to the shelf. He sniffed the pie.

"Eat!" Huey commanded.

Spunky's tail hung down. He walked away.

"Spunky doesn't even want it!" Huey said.

"What does a dog know about apple pie?" Latisha said. "This pie has almost exactly what's in apple pie. It has flour, and sugar, and apples. And you said you'd eat it. You promised!"

"We changed our minds. We won't eat it," Julian said.

"You have to!" Latisha said. Before we could answer her, she ran out of the playhouse. And then she locked the door.

She came around and stood by the window, with the shiny gold key in her hand.

"You locked us in!" Julian shouted.

"That's not fair!" I shouted.

"I said you could play in my playhouse if you ate my apple pie. And you promised. So eat it, promise-breakers!"

Latisha walked away, right back into her real house, and turned on the TV.

"We are prisoners!" Julian said.

Spunky whined and lay down on the floor. Huey touched the pie with his finger. In the sticky stuff, an apple slice moved. "It does have apples. It's creamy," he said.

"We could eat it," Julian said. "We did promise."

I touched the pie and licked my finger. "It's paste! Paste pie!" I said. "If Spunky won't eat it, we shouldn't!"

"How long do you think Latisha will keep us in here?" Huey said.

"I don't know," I said.

We sat down on the floor by the door.

Julian put his eye to the keyhole.

"This isn't such a good lock," he said. "Maybe I can open it."

He took his camping knife out of his pocket. It had a long special tool, like a toothpick. Julian stuck that into the lock. He tilted it and turned it, and finally the lock made a clicking sound.

We pushed on the door. It opened.

We took the pie with us when we left. I carried it up onto Latisha's porch steps. "Latisha, we have something for you," I called sweetly. We dumped the whole pie upside down on the steps. And then we ran.

In about a block we stopped running.

"I guess she won't play with us now," Huey said.

"Her mom won't like the mess on the steps," Julian said.

"Latisha can clean it up, she'll have to," I said.

"What if she doesn't?" Huey said. "What if she tells her mom or dad? And her folks tell our folks that we dumped that pie?"

"We were right to dump it!" I said.

"Maybe we better talk to Dad," Huey said.

"I don't want to," Julian said.

"We don't have to tell him what happened,"

Huey said. "We can just hint. And then we'll find out what he thinks."

We went down to Mr. Bates's shop. In the garage, he has a little refrigerator. He got us each an orange drink, and we sat down with him in his office.

"What's new?" he asked.

"Nothing," Julian said.

"Nothing at all," I said.

There was a silence.

"What would you think," Huey said, "if some people did something they shouldn't do, but they had a reason?"

"What people?" Mr. Bates said.

"Just—some people," Huey said. "Just—anybody."

"Hmmm," Mr. Bates said. He sipped his orange drink. "It would depend on the reason—and on what the people did."

"Well—say they dumped a pie on somebody's steps. That's all," Huey said.

"Did somebody dump a pie on our steps?" Mr. Bates asked.

"Not exactly," Julian said.

Mr. Bates set his orange-drink can down on his desk. It made a tiny crash.

"*Who* dumped pie on *whose* steps?" he demanded.

"We—" Huey said. "We dumped a pie on Latisha's steps."

"You *what*?" Mr. Bates yelled, and his eyebrows jumped about an inch.

"Dumped a pie. Just a very *small* pie," Julian said. "Practically no pie at all."

"It's practically like nobody dumped *anything*," Huey explained. "It's almost like something that practically didn't even happen!"

"Except that this very, very tiny pie got dumped," I said, "and it was us that did it."

Mr. Bates bit his lip, the way he does when he is trying to make himself be patient.

"And you had a reason," he said. "What was it?"

"The reason we did it is this. Latisha tried to make us eat raw pie, and when we wouldn't, she locked us in her playhouse!" Julian began. And then all of us explained the promise, and everything that happened, and Mr. Bates never got mad, he only listened till we finished.

"Do you think we were wrong to dump the pie?" Julian said.

"Yes, you were wrong," Mr. Bates said. "But I can see why you did it."

"Do you think we should have eaten her pie?" Huey asked. "We promised we would eat her pie and we didn't. Now we are promise-breakers."

"Hmmm," said Mr. Bates. And he thought awhile, like he was thinking about a big detective case.

"First of all, you should never keep a promise to do something that is bad for you. You thought you were going to get a real pie. When you made the promise, you didn't have all the facts. So you were right to break your promise."

"Good!" Julian said. "We were right!"

"But, second of all," Mr. Bates said, "you were wrong to make a promise without understanding it completely. It's not good to make a promise when you can't be absolutely sure you are willing to keep it."

Huey looked sad. "So we were wrong," he said. "Maybe we just should have eaten Latisha's pie. Then we would still be friends, maybe."

Mr. Bates took a sip of orange drink and stretched out his legs. He rubbed a hand across his eyes, as if he was trying to clear them to look into the future.

"Today, paste pie. Tomorrow, toad pie," he said.

"Toad pie!" Julian said. "Do you think Latisha would make us eat toad pie?"

"I don't know. What I think is, when people are being mean, and you don't stop them, they just get meaner." Mr. Bates tapped on his empty orange-drink can with his fingers, like it was a way to send secret messages.

"I don't know why, but Latisha is being mean to you. You have to find out why to make her stop."

"She doesn't have any reason to be mean!" Julian said.

"Maybe she does and we just don't know it," Huey said.

"Anyhow, she was wrong to be mean like that!" I said.

"But you all were mean, too, when you dumped the pie," Mr. Bates said. "I think you should help Latisha clean it up. And then ask her why she did the things she did."

Latisha was wiping her porch step with a rag. She looked as if she had been crying.

I was going to say, "Why are you so mean?" but instead I said, "Are you all right?"

"Yes," Latisha said. She sniffed.

"We'll help you clean up," Julian said. He took Latisha's rag and rinsed it at the faucet in the yard. He scrubbed the steps.

"Latisha," Huey said, "why did you give us paste pie? Why did you treat us so mean?"

"I like to pretend cook," Latisha said. "I always wanted somebody to eat my pretend cooking."

"But you locked us in! Why did you do that?" I asked.

Latisha stuck her chin out angrily. "Because you think I am a sissy!"

"A sissy?" Julian said. "I never said that!"

"We never called you that, either," Huey and I said.

"You think what I like is sissy!" Latisha said. "I like to play house, and you won't! You only want to do the same old stuff you always did before I moved here!"

I looked at Huey and Huey looked at me. We both looked at Julian.

Julian put down the rag. "Nobody ever told me you wanted to play house! I never knew."

"Gloria and Huey said—" Latisha began.

"Not to ask you," I finished.

"What do they know?" Julian said. "I never did play house, but I could do it."

"You could?" I said. I was surprised.

"You will?" Latisha said.

"Sure," Julian said.

"I will, too," I said.

"So will I," Huey said.

Julian threw his shoulders back and stood up very straight. For a second he looked very tall, almost as tall as Mr. Bates.

"You all can be whoever you want," he said. "I'll be the dad."

Spunky's Obsession

Huey's dog Spunky always used to be glad to see us—especially Huey, but also Julian and Latisha and me. When he saw us, he'd get so happy he'd jump on us and lick our faces. We didn't mind. We kind of liked it.

Then one day he jumped up on Mr. Bates. Mr. Bates was wearing his new white pants. Spunky wanted to lick Mr. Bates's face, but Mr. Bates was way too tall.

And Mr. Bates was mad. "Down!" he growled, like a big angry wolf.

Spunky didn't know the word "down." He just stayed where he was, grinning at Mr. Bates.

Mr. Bates shoved Spunky away. He tried to brush the paw prints off his pants. The paw prints wouldn't come off.

Spunky hung his head.

"That jumping is not good!" Mr. Bates said.

"We—we call it dancing," Huey said. "Spunky can do it a long time. He likes to dance."

"Some people don't like to be danced with," Mr. Bates said, "and I am one. Huey, you have to train that dog!"

"How?" Huey said.

"Teach simple commands," Mr. Bates said. "Start with 'Down!' And after that teach 'Sit!' and 'Stay!'"

Mr. Bates got a box of doggie biscuits out of his truck.

"Just teach him one command at a time," he said. "It might take him a whole day or more to learn one thing. When he does something right," he said, "give him lots of praise, and, sometimes, one of these."

"We'll help you, Huey," Julian said.

We went to the Bateses' back yard, in the shade under the oak trees. Up in the branches, squirrels were playing. They looked happy not being trained.

Latisha thought of how we could start training. We could show Spunky what the command "Down!" meant.

She told Huey, Julian, and me, "Down," and we lay down on the grass. Then we got up and Latisha told us "Down!" again. We did it five times.

Spunky sat and watched. His droopy velvet ears raised up when Latisha offered us doggie biscuits.

We wouldn't take any. "Spunky already knows that part!" Julian said.

Latisha put the biscuits away. Spunky's ears flopped back to normal.

"You saw what we did. Now you do it!" Huey said to Spunky. "Down!" he added.

Spunky looked at Huey. He didn't move.

"We're going to have to *make* him lie down," I said.

We acted together. When Huey said "Down," Julian and I pushed on Spunky's rump, and Latisha pulled his front paws out from under him.

Spunky went down with a soft thump. He looked surprised.

"Good dog!" Huey said.

We all petted Spunky.

Spunky looked happy and banged his tail against the grass. He knew he'd done something right. He just wasn't sure what it was.

A week went by. We repeated "Down!" to Spunky a lot of times, and finally when he heard the word he lay down by himself. And then we taught him "Sit!" and started on "Stay!"

It was when we got to "Stay!" that the squirrels made fun of him. When he stayed, they dropped acorns on his head. And they jeered "Chuh! Chuh! Chuh!" every time we said "Good dog!"

We didn't know exactly what "Chuh!" meant in squirrel language, except it sounded like an insult. Spunky thought it was an insult, too. Whenever he heard "Chuh!" he started answering "Yerf! Yerf! Yerf!"

Then one afternoon when he was staying in one place without moving, just the way he was supposed to, a squirrel got more insulting.

It came headfirst down the trunk of an oak tree and looked at Spunky. It raised its chin and said the loudest "Chuh!" we ever heard.

Spunky forgot "Stay!" He jumped up and sprang against the oak tree. The squirrel sneaked just out of reach.

"Chuh!" it said again, and Spunky went crazy. He ran all around the tree trunk, jumping and barking. Then a lot more squirrels in high branches said "Chuh!" and Spunky ran around with his nose in the air, looking for them, shouting "Yerf!" All the time we were calling "Spunky, come!" and "Down!" and "Sit!" but the only word Spunky listened to was "Chuh!"

Finally, he got really tired and lay down under the tree. Huey tried to talk to Spunky and get him to eat a doggie biscuit, but he wouldn't. He just stared up into the trees and whined.

We ran into the house and told Mrs. Bates.

She looked at Spunky out the kitchen window.

"That dog doesn't even move!" she marveled. "He is obsessed."

"Obsessed? What does that mean?" Huey asked.

"When a person can only think of just one thing and neglects everything else, that person is obsessed," Mrs. Bates explained. "I never heard of an obsessed dog before, but that's what Spunky is."

"Maybe he wants to be Lord of the Jungle," I said.

"Maybe so," Mrs. Bates said. "But, poor fellow, he'll never make it."

For a whole week Spunky wouldn't listen to any commands, or eat any doggie biscuits, or move. We had to bring him his water bowl and his puppy chow. He sat under the oak tree till he had worn a bare place in the grass, listening to "Chuh! Chuh!" and barking back "Yerf!" till he was hoarse.

By Saturday, Mr. Bates decided Spunky's condition was serious.

"I thought he would get over this," Mr. Bates said, "but he hasn't. Maybe he needs a change of scene."

"We try to move him, but he won't move!" Huey said.

"He will if you put his choke collar and his leash on him and pull," Mr. Bates said.

So we did. Spunky didn't want to go anywhere, but when the collar got too tight, he had to. We half walked him, half dragged him down the sidewalk. His eyes looked like muddy marbles, and he kept looking back toward home.

We got him to the park and rested near the river, where the bank is high and steep. Huey loosened Spunky's collar.

Spunky made a little snorting sound. He sniffed the air. He pushed a dandelion with his nose and ate a piece of grass.

His eyes started to get little sparks of life in them.

"I think we can let him free," I said. "I think he is forgetting his obsession."

Huey took his leash and collar off. Spunky wagged his tail and—

"Chuh!"

There was a squirrel between us and the river, sitting up and holding a nut in his front paws.

Spunky didn't even say "Yerf!" He just sprang. The squirrel ran.

"Oh no!" Latisha yelled. "He's going to get this one!"

The squirrel ran fast, but Spunky ran faster.

They raced to the river. Just when it looked like Spunky would catch him for sure, the squirrel dodged to a willow tree. Spunky didn't make the turn.

Ker-plash!

We ran.

Spunky was swimming in circles under the willow tree. His ears floated beside him like little boats.

The squirrel was out on a branch over Spunky's head, saying "Chuh!"

Whenever Spunky could get his breath, he was saying "Yerf!" like crazy.

"Spunky's obsessed again!" Huey said.

"Worse than ever!" Julian said.

We watched.

Spunky kept swimming round and round. The squirrel crept his way out along the willow branch. He made the branch bounce with every "Chuh!"

"Spunky-y-y-y!" Huey called.

Spunky paid no attention. He looked like a robot dog.

"Maybe he doesn't even know what land is anymore," Latisha said. "Maybe he's forgotten."

"I'll get him, I'll make him remember!" I said.

I pulled off my shoes and socks. I rolled up my pants legs. I jumped down the bank and waded into the river.

Spunky's eyes looked like marbles again, and his front legs churned like eggbeaters. I grabbed them high, up near his chest.

"Spunky, life is more than squirrels!" I shouted. And then I pulled him to shore, and Huey and Julian hauled him up onto the river-bank, and Spunky flopped down on the grass.

He panted as if he would never get enough air.

"Spunky, remember me! I'm Huey!" Huey said, and Spunky licked his hand.

"Chuh!" said the squirrel in the willow tree.

"Don't listen!" Huey begged.

"Don't let a squirrel's mind mess up your mind!" I said.

Spunky didn't look for the squirrel. He acted like he didn't even hear it. Then he stood, and shook himself hard, and sprayed water all over us.

We backed away. He shook himself some more, as if he was shaking squirrels out of his hair forever.

"That one tricked you, didn't he?" I said. "You found out you aren't King of the Jungle, didn't you?"

Spunky whined and licked my hand.

"Do you remember anything from before, Spunky?" Latisha asked. "Like—'Down!' "

Spunky looked blank.

"Down, Spunky!" Huey said, and slowly Spunky lay down on the grass.

"Stay, Spunky!" Huey said.

We tiptoed away. Spunky stayed right where he was.

"Good dog!" Huey said. "Come, Spunky!"

Huey clapped his hands and Spunky ran to us.

His eyes looked golden again.

"Good, good, *good* dog!" we said, and Spunky was so happy that he jumped for joy and licked our faces.

He stood on his hind legs and put big wet paws around Huey. He danced with Huey, and then he danced with all of us, just the way he used to. We didn't even think about dancing not being a command, or care about his paw prints on our clothes.

The Secret

Mr. Bates was on vacation, sitting on the steps in the sun. Huey, Julian, Latisha, and I were in the yard, working with Spunky. It wasn't his best day. He was on vacation, too. Sometimes he would do what we said. Sometimes he wouldn't. He was worst with Huey.

"He doesn't care about a word you say, Huey!" Latisha said. "And he is your dog!"

Huey looked sad. "He does too care!" he said.

"Huey," Mr. Bates said. "Let's get Spunky a new flavor of doggie biscuits!"

Huey and his dad went into the house together. When they came out, Mr. Bates sat down on the steps again, and Huey came over to us with fish-flavored doggie biscuits.

"I bet you I can make Spunky do *exactly* what I say," Huey told us.

"With fish-flavored doggie biscuits?" Julian said. "I doubt it."

"The secret is not just doggie biscuits," Huey said.

"He got bored with training. No matter what, today he won't do what you say," Latisha said.

"Yes, he will. He'll do it right now!" Huey said. "I'll bet you all ice-cream cones!"

Huey's eyes danced. He looked as if he knew something we didn't.

Latisha said, "I don't want to bet."

"Me either," Julian said.

Huey looked disappointed.

"I'll take your bet," I said.

Huey patted Spunky. He scratched him behind his ears. He knelt in front of Spunky and looked deep into his eyes. He muttered something to Spunky that we couldn't hear. Then he stood up.

Spunky bit at a flea. His mind seemed far away.

"Huey's going to lose!" I whispered to Latisha.

"Spunky," Huey said, in a very deep voice, "you must obey. Either sit—or don't!"

Spunky started to sit. Then he looked confused. He lay down and rolled over, waving his legs and rubbing his back against the grass.

"Good dog, Spunky!" Huey said. "See! He did just what I said. Gloria, I win!"

He gave Spunky a fish-flavored doggie biscuit. Spunky chomped it down.

I was not happy. "Huey, this bet is all differ-

ent from what I thought it was. There's no way you could lose!"

"That's right," Huey said.

I felt my pocket. I had money, but not enough to buy ice-cream cones for everybody.

Mr. Bates strolled over to us.

"It's not fair!" I said.

"What's not fair?" Mr. Bates asked.

"Mr. Bates," I said, "I just made a bet with Huey, but I didn't know what it really meant. And I lost."

"What did you bet?" Mr. Bates asked.

"Ice-cream cones for everybody!" I said. "And I have money only for two."

"Hmmm," Mr. Bates said. He felt in his pocket.

"I bet I have money for ice-cream cones," he said.

None of us wanted to bet against him. Especially me.

He opened the door of his truck for all of us to climb in.

"Can Spunky behave on a ride downtown?" he asked.

"I think so," Huey said, and Spunky barked yes.

We all got in the truck. Spunky sat on Huey's lap and stuck his head out the window. We started down the street. Air blew in the windows, and Spunky's ears flew like flags.

"We'll cruise on down Main Street," Mr. Bates said. "You all can pick the ice-cream place. And when we go in—Gloria, be ready!"

"Be ready?" I squeaked.

"That's right," Mr. Bates said. "Be ready. And either you pay—or I will."

The Question

I had a cold. I had to stay in bed for three days.

None of my friends called. Latisha didn't. Julian didn't. The first two days I didn't even care. The third day I felt better. I started to care.

I thought about Julian. Probably he was playing with Latisha. I started wondering if he liked Latisha better than me.

My mom came into my room with soup.

"By the way, I just saw Julian and Latisha,"

she said. "I told them you were sick. They said to tell you 'hi.' They hope you get better soon."

"What were they playing? Where were they going?" I asked.

"I don't know, Gloria," my mom said. She set down the soup. "Be careful with this, it's hot."

"Mom," I said, "do you think Julian likes Latisha better than me?"

"Probably not," my mom said, "but I don't know what he thinks. Did he do something that makes you think he doesn't like you?"

"No," I said. "But—"

"Lying here sick has got you worrying for nothing," my mom said.

"It's not for nothing," I said. "See, the way it used to be was Julian and I were best friends. But now Latisha is always with us. And it's not the same."

My mom sat down on the edge of my bed. "Gloria," she said, "would you really want Julian to like you best just because you were the only friend he had? That's what you're saying, really."

"It was nicer before," I said.

"Gloria," my mom said, "wanting one person all to yourself isn't wanting a friend. It's wanting a prisoner!"

"I don't want Julian to be my prisoner," I told her. "I just want him to like me best."

"If you want him to like you best, you'll have to let him be free," my mom said.

"He *is* free," I said. "I just want to know who he likes better. When I'm well, I'm going to ask him!"

"Ask him if you want," my mom said. "But remember, it may not work."

"It will!" I said. "Julian always tells me everything!"

"Don't be too sure," my mom said. "Sometimes people don't want to say what they feel. Sometimes they don't tell the truth. There is an old saying, Gloria: 'Actions speak louder than words.' Watch Julian's actions, and you can guess how he feels."

"But I don't want to guess!" I said. "I want to *know!*"

My mom sighed. "You'll have to do things your own way, I suppose. Just don't expect it to work out the way you want."

I frowned and pulled my covers up to my neck.

My mom smoothed my covers. She smoothed my forehead.

"Gloria," she said, "there isn't a measuring stick you can put to friendship. When you start measuring too much, it's like digging up a plant in the garden to see how it's growing. If you dig it up too many times, it will die."

"Friendships die?" I said.

"Sometimes," my mom said. "But then new ones grow."

"I want the ones I have now!" I said.

"Listen, Gloria," my mom said. "This is a hard truth, but I am going to tell it to you anyway. Friends come and go, but your best friend is always you. As long as *you* like you, lots of other people will, and deep down you'll be happy."

I sat up. My bed jiggled my bedside table, and the table jiggled my soup. My mom moved the table away from the bed.

"How can I be my best friend?" I said. "I'm only just one person!"

"You need to learn to talk to yourself," my mom said. "For instance, you might say to yourself, 'I know you're tired of being sick, and it's not your fault that you're sick, and you're very good and patient not to complain.' Like that," my mom explained.

My mom went back to her work, and I ate my soup. Afterward, I tried being my best friend. I thanked myself for eating all my soup, and I told myself that I was a nice person even if I was sick, and that I liked me very, very much. I thought some more about Julian, and then I fell asleep.

In the morning I was better. My mom said I could go out. I got dressed and tied red ribbons on my braids. I started down the sidewalk to Julian's house.

One of me practiced saying, "By the way" in the cool, casual way my mom says it. "By the way. By the way. By the way."

The other me, the best-friend one, was talking, too. "You are a very, very, *very* nice person," she told me, "and I like you very much—even if you are going to do something very very dumb."

I saw Huey walking Spunky to the park.

When I got to the Bateses' house, Julian was in the yard.

"Gloria! Come see what I found!" he called.

We went to the hedge by the driveway, and he pointed.

The first time I ever met Julian, he showed me a bird's nest in the hedge. Now, almost in the same spot, there was a new nest, and four baby birds were in it. They were nice to see, but they weren't pretty.

"They hardly have any feathers!" I said.

"You know why?" Julian said. "It's because they're just born. And they can't have feathers when they're inside their eggshells, because there isn't enough space there. So they grow the feathers later. And everything is like that!"

"What do you mean?" I asked.

"There's an order and a reason to everything. That's what my dad says. Sometimes

you can't see it right away, but sometimes you can.

"I thought of showing the baby birds to Latisha," he continued, "but I wanted to show you first."

"Why?" I said. I crossed my fingers. I hoped Julian would say, "Because I like you best."

"A lot of reasons," Julian said. "For one thing, Latisha wants me to help her start a zoo. And these babies shouldn't be in a zoo! I'm not showing them to Latisha till they can fly."

"Oh," I said. I was disappointed. Julian was not telling me what I wanted to find out.

We took a step back from the nest. "By the way," I said.

"By the way what?" Julian repeated.

"Oh, just—by the way."

"There is something you are not saying!" Julian said. "Say it!"

"By the way," I mumbled, "who do you like better, me or Latisha?"

"Oh, no!" Julian shouted. He covered his ears and his eyes with his hands.

"I only just asked," I said.

"That's what Latisha did, too," Julian said. "She only just asked."

"Asked who you like better?"

"Right!" Julian said. He scowled.

"And—um, by the way, what did you tell her?" I said very calm-like.

"I told her I wouldn't tell her."

"You wouldn't tell! Why not?"

"A person needs some secrets," Julian said. "A person without secrets is not a person."

"But you could tell me this little one," I said.

"No!" Julian said. "If I told Latisha I liked you better, she would be mad. If I told you I liked Latisha better, you would be mad. I am not telling anything to anybody!"

"That's not fair, because—" I said.

"Who do you like better, me or Shavaun?" Julian interrupted.

"That's not fair!" I said. I felt strange. I always liked Julian more than anybody, but the minute he asked about our friend Shavaun, I wasn't sure.

"You don't know what you think," Julian said scornfully, "but I know what I think. Latisha tried to trick me into eating paste pie, but I like her anyway. Right now you are pestering me, but I still like you anyway."

"You think Latisha and I are just the same!" I felt very bad.

"Well, not exactly," Julian said. "So far, Latisha likes me if I do things she wants me to do. But, so far, you like me when I'm just me. And that's nice."

I smiled. "And you like me when I'm just me," I said. "And *that's* nice."

We didn't say anything then. We just watched the baby birds till the parent birds came to feed them. The parents must have cared a lot about their babies, they fed them so fast and well.

It didn't matter to them which baby was prettier. What mattered was, they were growing. One day, all of them would fly.

A Rock in the Road

I had a bad day at school. Afterward, I walked home with Latisha and Julian and Huey.

I said, "Julian, do you understand fractions?"

"Sure," Julian said.

"Fractions are easy," Latisha said.

The way she said it made me mad.

"Fractions are phony!" I said.

"What do you mean, phony?" Julian asked.

"For instance," I said, "one half, one divided by two. Two *can't* go into one. One is littler than two."

"Two *can* go into one!" Latisha argued.

"It seems to me it can't," Huey said.

"You don't know," Julian said. "You're not in our grade."

"Two can go into one because a person can write it down," Latisha said. "You saw Mr. Burns do it."

"A person can write anything down," I said. "I can write down, 'I am a giraffe,' but that doesn't make it true!"

"Fractions don't have anything to do with giraffes!" Latisha said. "Anyhow, Julian and I get fractions. Probably you will, too, in time."

I suppose she meant to be nice, but I didn't take it nice.

I saw a stone in front of me. I kicked it hard. It always feels good to kick a stone in the road and watch it roll. But then it stops rolling, and you feel just the way you did before.

Julian, Huey, and Latisha went on down the street. I went into my house. It felt empty.

My mom was gone. She was out of town on a business trip. It was the first time she ever went away overnight without my dad and me.

My dad was supposed to take care of me, but I didn't know if he could. I didn't know if he could braid my hair. Also, I never saw him cook. I was scared of what we might have to eat.

I watered the plants, the way I promised my mom I would. Then I opened my math book and stared at the picture on the unit "Discovering Fractions." A boy and a girl were smiling, standing on one foot and holding up fractions in their hands as if it was a big game. They reminded me of Julian and Latisha.

"It is a big game, all right," I told them in my mind. "Two won't go into one!"

I started drawing pictures of fractions in my notebook. Whale into robin; elephant into flea; buffalo into puppy; sun into lightbulb; ocean into water drop; volcano into anthill.

Then I drew big smoke and fire clouds all over the volcano and lots of ants swarming around the anthill. That's what I was doing when my dad came home.

He gave me a hug and looked at my paper.

"What are you working on? Art?" he asked.

"Not exactly," I said.

"How about corn bread and tuna salad for dinner?" he said.

"You know how to make corn bread?" I said.

"Of course," he said.

"With Mom's recipe?" I said.

"No, with my own recipe," he said.

I set the table and he made dinner. Nothing tasted the way my mom made it, but it tasted good.

"Do you know how to braid hair?" I said.

"Of course," he said.

"Like Mom does?" I asked.

"No, my way," he said.

"How did you learn it?" I said.

"I used to braid your Aunt Vanessa's. When she was little. I'm good at it," he added. "You'll see in the morning."

After dinner, my dad washed dishes and I dried. It felt nice to be with him.

"How was school today?" he asked.

I wanted to tell him it wasn't fine, but I couldn't. Because he would think I should understand fractions and I didn't.

"It was fine," I said.

I am not used to talking to my dad. I practically never talk to him, because there is no time.

The reason is Quick Kitchens. Quick Kitchens is my dad's business. All day long, he works in other people's houses, installing new kitchens. When he comes home, he is tired. Then, after dinner, he goes to the answering machine. He plays back all the messages on it about Quick Kitchens, and then he returns the people's calls.

"How much time do you spend in your kitchen?" he asks them. They answer something I can't hear, and then he says, "Once you install a Quick Kitchen, you'll finish your kitchen chores in a fraction of the time."

I didn't used to know what "fraction" meant, but I still hated it. To me it was just a poor word that kept getting hauled out and dragged around and dragged around till it was all worn out.

"Well, I'm glad school was good," my dad said. He rinsed the last dish and I dried it.

"Thanks for helping," he said. "Time to go check the machine."

In a second he would click the answering machine on. In a second all the new Quick Kitchen messages would start pouring out into our old kitchen and he would write down all the numbers to call back. And I would never talk to him.

"Daddy!" I said.

"What, honey?"

I wouldn't have said it like I did, but it just spilled out.

"I hate Quick Kitchens!" I said. "I hate listening to the answering machine. I hate the people's voices, and I hate it when you call them back, and I hate it when you say, 'You will finish your kitchen chores in a fraction of the time.' "

My dad stayed very quiet. I was scared that he was mad.

Then he reached out and took my hand. "I get sick of Quick Kitchens myself, sometimes," he said softly. "Let's you and me sit down and talk."

We sat down at the kitchen table.

"I have to answer the calls," my dad explained. "It's how I get new business. I will try not to say things the same way all the time. I make so many calls, after a while I don't even hear myself."

"It just keeps going on and on," I said.

"Sometimes life is like that," my dad said. "But change always comes."

"Another thing," I said. "I am stupid and I hate fractions. I don't understand them, and I'm the only one in my math class who doesn't get them, and I don't even know why."

I put my head down on the table. My dad lifted it up.

"Gloria," he said. "You're not stupid."

"Then why don't I get it?"

"Everybody has things they don't get," my dad said.

"Everybody?" I repeated. It seemed there must be somebody who got absolutely everything—but for sure it wasn't me.

"It's like this," my dad said. "Everybody's got a different road in life. And for a while you may go along your road just fine, and then all of a sudden there's a rock—a rock so big you can't get by. You can't climb over it, you can't go around it. All you can do is just stand and study it and think and think and think. And then, all of a sudden, you understand it. And then that rock disappears and you can move again."

"Julian doesn't have a rock in his road. Latisha doesn't have a rock in her road," I said.

"You don't know," my dad said. "Everyone does at one time or another. It may not be fractions, but it will be something."

"Fractions is a rock that won't disappear," I said. "Fractions is going to be the next two months, at least."

"Fractions won't disappear," my dad said, "but when you understand them, they won't be a rock in your road. They will be different.

Just a pebble or a grain of sand that you'll pass by."

"What I don't get," I said, "is this."

I got my homework notebook, and I wrote "1/4."

"Four cannot go into one," I said. "It won't fit."

"Think of it this way," my dad said. "Think of that as meaning 'one of four.' "

"Give me your right hand," he said.

I did, and he held my index finger.

"This finger is one of five," he said. "Correct?"

"Yes," I said.

"It's one-fifth of your fingers on that hand," he said. "Right?"

"Right!"

"Now give me your left hand," my dad said, so I did.

"If you include both hands, this same finger

is one of ten. What part of all your fingers is it?"

"One-tenth," I said.

"Right," he said.

We went on adding up finger fractions until that got too easy and my dad started counting in my toes. We talked about twentieths then, and I still could do it.

"See," he said, "it's not so hard. Look how you're dissolving that big rock in your road. To-morrow night, we can work on it some more."

He started to get up from the table, but I didn't want him to go.

"About those rocks," I said. "Did you have rocks in your road when you were a kid?"

"Sure," my dad said.

"Is it just kids that have them?"

"No, everybody," my dad said.

"Do you have them now?"

"Yes," my dad answered.

"Like what?" I asked.

"Quick Kitchens," my dad said. "Quick Kitchens doesn't leave me time to spend with you and your mom. Quick Kitchens is a rock."

"But you're going to get around it?" I said.

"I'm working on it," my dad said. "I'm thinking on it. It will take time. But one day that great big rock in my road won't be there anymore."

My dad got up. I thought he was going to start making calls, and maybe he was, but then he changed his mind.

"Maybe I'm pushing that rock too hard," he said, "and maybe I'll get some new ideas if I take time off from all that pushing. Gloria, do you want to play checkers?"

"Yes!" I said, and I got the board out.

We played three games and I won twice. Then it was my bedtime.

I got ready for bed, amazed how things aren't hardly ever the way I think they are.

My dad came into my room. He kissed me good night.

"Daddy, I always thought you *loved* Quick Kitchens!" I said. "You really don't?"

And my dad said, "I don't love Quick Kitchens. I love you."